ASTERIX AND CAESAR'S GIFT

TEXT BY GOSCINNY

DRAWINGS BY UDERZO

TRANSLATED BY ANTHEA BELL AND DEREK HOCKRIDGE

DARGAUD CANADA Ltée
307 BENJAMIN-HUDON ST-LAURENT MONTREAL P.Q. H4N1J1

ASTERIX THROUGHOUT THE WORLD

Australia	Hodder and Stoughton Children's Books, 47 Bedford Square, London WC1B 3DP, England
Austria	Delta Verlag, Postfach 1215, 7 Stuttgart 1, German Federal Republic
Belgium	Dargaud Benelux, 3, rue Kindermans, 1050 Brussels, Belgium
Brazil	Cedibra, rue Filomena Nunes 162, Rio de Janeiro, Brazil
Denmark	Gutenberghus Bladene, Vognmagergade 11, 1148 Copenhagen Denmark
Federal German Republic	Delta Verlag, Postfach 1215, 7 Stuttgart 1, Federal German Republic
Finland	Sanoma Osakeyhtio, Ludviginkatu 2-10, 00130 Helsinki 13, Finland
France	Dargaud Editeur, 12, rue Blaise-Pascal, 92201 Neuilly-sur-Seine, France
France (Regional Editions)	Breton : Armor Diffusion, 59, rue Duhamel, 35100 Rennes, France Langue d'Oc : Société Toulousaine du Livre, avenue de Larrieu, 31094 Toulouse, France
Holland	Dargaud Benelux, 3, rue Kindermans, 1050 Brussels, Belgium Oberon b.v., Ceylonpoort 5-25, Haarlem, Netherlands (distribution)
Hong Kong	Hodder and Stoughton Children's Books, 47 Bedford Square, London WC1B 3DP, England
Iceland	Fjolvi HF, Njorvasund 15a, Reykjavik, Iceland
Indonesia	Yayasan Aspirasi Pemuda, Jalan Kebon Kacang, Raya 1, Flat 3, Tingkat 111, Jakarta, Indonesia
Italy	Arnoldo Mondadori Editore, via Bianca de Savoia 20, 20122 Milan, Italy
Jugoslavia	Nip Forum, Vojvode Misica 1-3, 2100 Novi Sad, Jugoslavia
New Zealand	Hodder and Stoughton Children's Books, 47 Bedford Square, London WC1B 3DP, England
Norway	A/S Hjemmet (Gutenberghus Group), Kristian den 4 des Gate 13, Oslo 1, Norway
Portugal	Meriberica, rue D. Filipa de Vilhena 4-5°, Lisbon 1, Portugal
Roman Empire	Delta Verlag, Postfach 1215, 7 Stuttgart 1, German Federal Republic
South Africa	Hodder and Stoughton Children's Books, 47 Bedford Square, London WC1B 3DP, England
Spain	Ediciones Junior S.A., 386 Aragon, Barcelona 9, Spain
Sweden	Hemmets Journal Forlag (Gutenberghus Group), Fack, 200 22 Malmo, Sweden
Switzerland	Interpress S.A., En Budron B, 1052 Le Mont/Lausanne, Switzerland (distribution)
Turkey	Kervan Kitabcilik, Serefendi Sokagi 31, Cagaloglu-Istamboul, Turkey
United Kingdom	Hodder and Stoughton Children's Books, 47 Bedford Square, London WC1B 3DP, England
Wales	Gwasg Y Dref Wen, 6 Rookwood Close, Llandaff, Cardiff, Wales, Great Britain

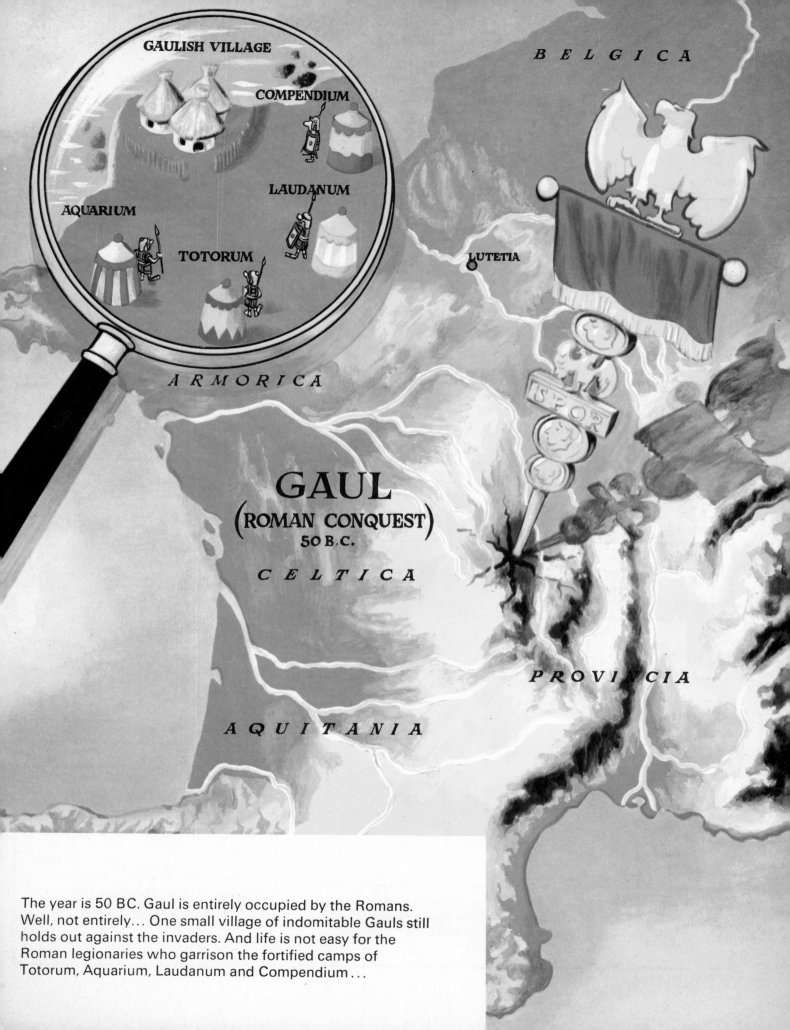

The year is 50 BC. Gaul is entirely occupied by the Romans. Well, not entirely… One small village of indomitable Gauls still holds out against the invaders. And life is not easy for the Roman legionaries who garrison the fortified camps of Totorum, Aquarium, Laudanum and Compendium…

a few of the Gauls

Asterix, the hero of these adventures. A shrewd, cunning little warrior; all perilous missions are immediately entrusted to him. Asterix gets his superhuman strength from the magic potion brewed by the druid Getafix…

Obelix, Asterix's inseparable friend. A menhir delivery-man by trade; addicted to wild boar. Obelix is always ready to drop everything and go off on a new adventure with Asterix – so long as there's wild boar to eat, and plenty of fighting.

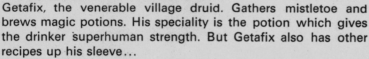

Getafix, the venerable village druid. Gathers mistletoe and brews magic potions. His speciality is the potion which gives the drinker superhuman strength. But Getafix also has other recipes up his sleeve…

Cacofonix, the bard. Opinion is divided as to his musical gifts. Cacofonix thinks he's a genius. Everyone else thinks he's unspeakable. But so long as he doesn't speak, let alone sing, everybody likes him…

Finally, Vitalstatistix, the chief of the tribe. Majestic, brave and hot-tempered, the old warrior is respected by his men and feared by his enemies. Vitalstatistix himself has only one fear; he is afraid the sky may fall on his head tomorrow. But as he always says, 'Tomorrow never comes.

SOON AFTERWARDS...

HOW LONG HAVE YOU DONE THEN, SON?

TWO YEARS.

ONLY EIGHTEEN MORE TO GO, SON, THE END'S IN SIGHT!

YES: THIS TIME XVIII YEARS WHERE SHALL I BE? NOT IN THE ROMAN INFANTRY!※

※ OLD ROMAN ARMY SONG, AN ADAPTATION OF WHICH IS STILL CURRENT IN ENGLISH SCHOOLS TODAY.

NEXT MORNING, IN JULIUS CAESAR'S PALACE...

WELL, CENTURION, SO SOME OF OUR VETERANS GET THEIR HONESTA MISSIO TODAY. ALL MEN WITH GOOD CONDUCT RECORDS, I HOPE?

YES, THEY'VE DONE FINE, O JULIUS CAESAR... BARRING ONE OLD SOAK WHO HASN'T BEEN SOBER IN TWENTY YEARS.

IN FACT HE'S IN THE GLASSHOUSE THIS VERY MOMENT. HE WAS USING INSULTING LANGUAGE ABOUT YOU LAST NIGHT.

INSULTING LANGUAGE, EH? WELL, I'VE GOT AN IDEA... WE'LL HAVE A SPOT OF FUN WITH HIM!

GET HIM OUT OF PRISON AND HAVE HIM LINED UP FOR THE PRESENTATION CEREMONY ALONG WITH THE REST.

YOU'RE GOING TO THROW HIM TO THE LIONS, O CAESAR?

WORSE! I'M GOING TO GIVE HIM A PRESENT!

SOME HOURS LATER...

ATTEN—SHUN!

②

LEGIO EXPEDITA!

HMM?

CLICK! CLICK! CLICK! CLICK! CLICK! CLICK!

HEY, YOU! LEGIO EXPEDITA!

OH...RIGHT....

LEGIONARIES, YOU HAVE COMPLETED YOUR TWENTY YEARS' MILITARY SERVICE. WITH THIS LITTLE FORMALITY BEHIND YOU, YOUR WHOLE LIFE LIES BEFORE YOU...

YOU HAVE SERVED ROME WELL, AND I AM GOING TO REWARD YOU BY GIVING YOU PLOTS OF LAND IN OUR COLONIES...

HERE ARE YOUR TITLE DEEDS TO LAND AT NEMAUSUS*...

* NÎMES

YOU HAVE BEEN ALLOTTED LAND NEAR ARELATUM*...

* ARLES

AND IT'S AQUAE SEXTIAE* FOR YOU...

* AIX

THIS IS THE MAN.

I'D NEVER HAVE GUESSED!

I'VE GOT SOMETHING SPECIAL FOR YOU... I'M GIVING YOU A LITTLE VILLAGE BY THE SEASIDE IN ARMORICA....

YOU ARE?

... A LITTLE GAULISH VILLAGE SURROUNDED BY FORTIFIED ROMAN CAMPS.

3

AVE, CLAUDIUS!

WE MUST HAVE A REUNION SOME TIME AND CHAT ABOUT THE GOOD OLD DAYS.

YES, WE'VE HAD SOME FUN, COME TO THINK OF IT!

REMEMBER THAT TIME I LOOKED THE OPTIO STRAIGHT IN THE EYE AND I SAID TO HIM, *QUI HABET AURES AUDIENDI, AUDIAT*, I SAID?

WHAT'S THE GOOD OF A GAULISH VILLAGE? CAN'T DRINK A GAULISH VILLAGE, CAN I?

HEY, EGGANLETTUS! WANT TO BUY A VILLAGE?

NO THANKS I'VE GOT A PLOT OF LAND NEAR NICAEA.✳ I'M GOING TO GROW SALAD STUFF.

✳ NICE

HAVE A NICE TIME IN ARMORICA, TREMENSDELIRIUS! AVE!

SCRATCH SCRATCH

SOME DAYS LATER, IN AN INN AT ARAUSIO✳ ON ROMAN ROAD VII

✳ ORANGE

WINE! MORE WINE, BY MERCURY!

YOU'VE HAD QUITE ENOUGH, AND IT'S CLOSING TIME. COME ON, PAY UP!

PAY?

PAY!.... HAHAHAHA!

I CAN'T PAY LANDLORD, I HAVEN'T GOT ANY MONEY!

WHAT?

NO, BUT LISTEN HERE! I HAVEN'T A SESTERTIUS TO MY NAME, BUT I'M RICH! GIVE ME SOME WINE AND I'LL GIVE YOU A WHOLE VILLAGE!

A VILLAGE?

THAT'S RIGHT, A VILLAGE! A LOVELY SEASIDE VILLAGE IN ARMORICA!

SEE THIS TABLET BEARING JULIUS CAESAR'S OWN SEAL?

4

You mean you'd give me this village, just for the price of a meal and a little wine?

I must ask my wife.

Don't forget the wine on your way back!

...And look at this! An official document! With Julius Caesar's own seal! I've always dreamt of owning land...

Well, Angina?

I must admit, it's tempting... The climate here doesn't really suit me, seaside air is so bracing, and what's more, an inn is no fit place to bring up a young girl...

...pecially as our little influenza was never happy 'bout leaving Lutetia to come here.

We could sell this inn...

Well?

It's a deal!

Fill it up!

As it happens... the little village which has changed hands for a hunk of bread and a few mugs of wine...

...IS THIS VILLAGE!

GAULISH VILLAGE

COMPENDIUM

AQUARIUM

LAUDANUM

TOTORUM

5

10

IT SEEMS TO BE INHABITED... THERE'S SMOKE RISING FROM THE CHIMNEYS...

HUH! WE'LL JUST TELL THE VILLAGERS TO LEAVE, AND THAT WILL BE THAT!

WHEN THEY SEE JULIUS CAESAR'S OFFICIAL SEAL THEY'LL GET THE BRACING SEA WIND UP ALL RIGHT!

WHY DON'T WE GO BACK TO LUTETIA? IT'S DEAD BORING IN THE COUNTRY!

NOBODY ASKED YOUR OPINION, ZAZA!

WUCHKORG!

SORRY ABOUT THAT. I'M TEACHING MY DOG TO RETRIEVE.

YOU GREAT PIGHEADED FOOL, I TOLD YOU THAT MENHIR WAS TOO BIG!

OF COURSE, NOTHING'S EVER QUITE RIGHT FOR MISTER ASTERIX, IS IT? FIRST MY DOG'S TOO SMALL, THEN MY MENHIR'S TOO BIG!

YOU'LL END UP KILLING SOMEONE WITH THAT MENHIR!

HUH! HEAR THAT? WHOEVER HEARD OF MENHIRS BEING DANGEROUS? MUSHROOMS, YES, BUT MENHIRS... WELL, I ASK YOU!

TH...THEY'RE CRAZY!

ER...DO YOU HAVE SOME SORT OF CHIEF HERE?

YES, WE DO HAVE SOME SORT OF CHIEF... YOU'LL FIND HIM IN THAT HOUSE OVER THERE.

DON'T LEAVE US ALONE AT THE MERCY OF THESE MADMEN!

ALL RIGHT, ALL RIGHT... BUT THEY'RE NOT MAD... JUST A LITTLE RUSTIC, MAYBE...

WOULD YOU KINDLY GO AND GET YOUR CHIEF? I HAVE SOME VERY IMPORTANT NEWS.

RIGHT.

WOOF! WOOF!

SOME VERY IMPORTANT NEWS? LET'S GO AND SEE WHAT'S UP!

I HAVE TO GO OUT, PEDIMENTA DEAR.

OH NO, YOU DON'T! THE WATER'S WARM, AND I'LL BE NEEDING THE TUB AFTERWARDS TO DO THE WASHING!

SOON AFTERWARDS...

OUR CHIEF VITALSTATISTIX!

JUST A BIT RUSTIC, EH?

WHO ARE YOU, AND WHAT DO YOU WANT?

MY NAME IS ORTHOPAEDIX, AND I MUST ASK YOU AND YOUR MEN TO LEAVE MY VILLAGE.

WHAT WAS THAT AGAIN?

I SAID THIS VILLAGE IS MINE, AND YOU MUST LEAVE, ALL YOU GAULS, WORTHY AS YOU MAY BE. I'M A MAN OF PROPERTY NOW...

??

TAP! TAP! TAP!

THIS PROPERTY, AND HERE ARE THE TITLE DEEDS.

BRING ME THAT TABLET.

RIGHT, CHIEF!

?

NO, DOWN HERE!

CLUCK

SEE THAT SIGNATURE?

HMPH? HAHA...

HAHAHAHAHAHA!

?

9

HERE WE ARE. THE CHIEF HAS GIVEN US THIS HOUSE FOR OUR INN.

UNHYGIENIX FR... ...ONGER

WHAT? YOU MEAN WE'VE LEFT OUR NICE INN AT ARAUSIO JUST TO OPEN ANOTHER IN THIS WRETCHED VILLAGE, WHEN THE WHOLE PLACE BELONGS TO US ANYWAY?

BUT THEY DON'T WANT TO GIVE US THE VILLAGE!

OH, LET'S GO BACK TO UNCLE DITHYRAMBIX IN LUTETIA!

NO. NO! WE SHALL BE VERY COMFORTABLE HERE... AND THE AIR'S SO BRACING!

BRACING? IT STINKS OF ROTTEN FISH!

SNIFF! SNIFF!

WE'LL AIR THE HOUSE OUT... ANYWAY, THAT'S THE SMELL OF THE SEA!

IT'S SOME TIME SINCE ANY FISH SMELLING LIKE THAT SAW THE SEA!

IT'S FUN HAVING NEW PEOPLE IN THE VILLAGE, ISN'T IT, GETAFIX?

WELL, I HAVE A NOTION WE SHAN'T BE BORED. EVERYONE'S TALKING ABOUT THEM, ANYWAY.

SHE'S ALMOST AS LIGHT AS YOU DOGMATIX!

GRRRRR!

OBÉLIX QUARRY

NEW PEOPLE? WHAT NEW PEOPLE?

YOU KNOW ME, I'VE GOT NOTHING AGAINST FOREIGNERS. SOME OF MY BEST FRIENDS ARE FOREIGNERS, BUT THESE PARTICULAR FOREIGNERS AREN'T FROM THIS VILLAGE!

AS FOR THAT GIRL, SHE HAS THE MOST APPALLING TASTE!

FUNNY SMELL HERE.

YOU THINK SO? I DON'T SMELL ANYTHING. I WAS AFRAID IT MIGHT SMELL OF FRYING, BUT NO....

SNIFF! SNIFF!

IMPEDIMENTA, MEET OUR NEW INNKEEPER, ORTHOPAEDIX.

AND THIS IS MY WIFE ANGINA.

PLEASED TO MEET YOU.

PLEASED TO MEET YOU.

NICE LITTLE PLACE YOU HAVE HERE, MRS ORTHOPAEDIX. WHAT A PITY ABOUT THE SMELL OF FISH.

FISH!

WE WERE OBLIGED TO TAKE WHAT OFFERED, MRS VITALSTATISTIX. DARE SAY YOUR PLAICE SMELLS BETTER.

NATURALLY, MRS ORTHOPAEDIX. AFTER ALL I'M THE CHIEF'S WIFE!

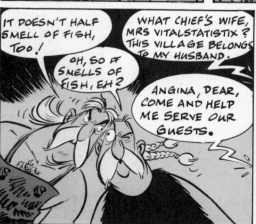
IT DOESN'T HALF SMELL OF FISH, TOO!

WHAT CHIEF'S WIFE, MRS VITALSTATISTIX? THIS VILLAGE BELONGS TO MY HUSBAND.

OH, SO IT SMELLS OF FISH, EH?

ANGINA, DEAR, COME AND HELP ME SERVE OUR GUESTS.

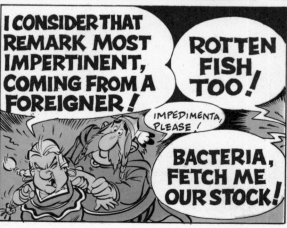
I CONSIDER THAT REMARK MOST IMPERTINENT, COMING FROM A FOREIGNER!

ROTTEN FISH TOO!

IMPEDIMENTA, PLEASE!

BACTERIA, FETCH ME OUR STOCK!

NO CARPING, FRIENDS! THIS ONE'S ON THE HOUSE MUSSEL IN!

BROMM! CRRACK! BING! TCHAC!

THE BRACING BREEZE

COMES THE DAWN...

COCK-A-DOODLE-DO...

DO STOP CRYING, MUMMY. ALL OUR GUESTS HAVE GONE.

BOOHOOHOO!

YOU WERE RIGHT, GINA DEAR, THEY *ARE* CRAZY! WE'RE LEAVING! I KNOW WHAT... WE'LL GO BACK TO LUTETIA!

GOODY!

OVER MY DEAD BODY! WE'RE STAYING HERE!

BUT... I THOUGHT AFTER LAST NIGHT'S PUNCH-UP.

PUNCH-UP? WHAT PUNCH-UP? IT'S THAT HORRIBLE WOMAN! SHE HUMILIATED ME! HER HOUSE IS OUR HOUSE!

AND THIS VILLAGE IS OUR VILLAGE! WE'VE GOT TO TURN THEM OUT OF HERE!

TURN OUT THE CHIEF? BUT I RATHER LIKE HIM...

AHEM...

(15)

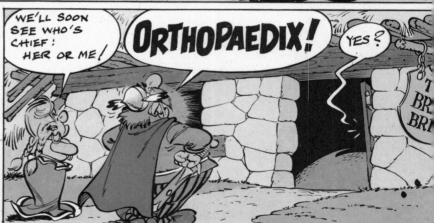

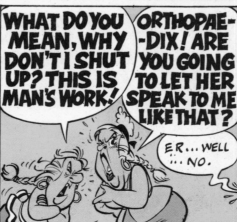

20

16

YOU WANTED ME, 'VITALSTATISTIX?

THAT'S RIGHT, CACOFONIX... I'VE GOT A LITTLE JOB FOR YOU...

IT'S NOT THAT I DOUBT THEIR LOYALTY, EXACTLY, BUT I'D LIKE YOU TO SOUND OUT OUR FRIENDS; SEE IF THEY WANT A CHANGE OF CHIEF.

LATER...

WELL, WHAT NEWS?

GERIATRIX IS BACKING YOU. HE SAYS HE'S GOT NOTHING AGAINST FOREIGNERS BUT THEY DON'T BELONG HERE. THE OTHERS DON'T MIND ONE WAY OR THE OTHER, SO LONG AS THEY STILL GET PLENTY OF BOARS AND ROMANS...

FULLIAUTOMATIX THOUGHT I WAS GOING TO SOUND HIM OUT IN SONG, SO HE KNOCKED ME OUT FIRST.

YOU HAVEN'T VOICED YOUR OWN OPINION YET...?

HUH! YOU DON'T LIKE MY VOICE ANY MORE THAN THE REST OF THEM!

WHAT, ME? I SIMPLY LOVE YOUR VOICE!

YOU DO? LISTEN TO THIS NEW PROTEST SONG I'VE JUST COMPOSED, THEN...

SPLOIING!

CLOIIK!

WE SHALL OVERCOME... WE SHALL OVER-COME...

FREEDOM FIGHTERS THE WORLD OVER OWE THIS SONG TO CACOFONIX. THE ORIGINAL TUNE HAS, OF COURSE, BEEN EXTENSIVELY REVISED...

STOP! I'M OVERCOME ALREADY! THIS IS A PROTEST... MARCH!

ALL RIGHT, ORTHOPAEDIX CAN HAVE THE BENEFIT OF MY SONG! MAYBE HE'LL APPRECIATE IT!!!

PEDIMENTA, I FEEL WE MAY HAVE MADE A MISTAKE... THAT'S ONE PROTEST VOTE ALREADY!

WHY NOT ADDRESS YOUR PEOPLE? ROUSE THEM UP A BIT?

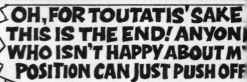

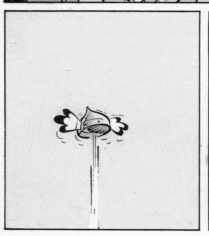

HERE'S ANOTHER!

OH, THANKS, OBELIX. I THINK THAT'S ENOUGH, DON'T YOU? WHY DON'T WE HAVE A LITTLE TALK?

WAIT! THERE ARE STILL A FEW MORE OVER THERE!

SNIFF! SNIFF!

YOU WANTED TO TALK TO ME?

YES, DO SIT DOWN... HERE, BESIDE ME.

I DO LIKE THIS VILLAGE AND THIS FOREST OBELIX...

... BUT IF DADDY DOESN'T GET ELECTED CHIEF WE'LL HAVE TO GO BACK TO LUTETIA ... ISN'T THAT SAD?

SNIFF!

SNIFF!

HALF A MINUTE! THERE'S SOMETHING MOVING OVER THERE!

IT WAS A ROMAN THIS TIME. YOU DO SOMETIMES GET THEM IN THE SUMMER MONTHS... THESE ROMANS ARE CRAZY!

21

WE'VE POPPED IN FOR A DRINK, AND HERE'S ONE OF OUR FISH, SINCE YOU SEEM TO LIKE THEM. WE KEEP THIS SORT FOR SPECIAL OCCASIONS.

'LL GO AND GET THE SPADE.

NEVER MIND HIM, HE'S ONLY JOKING... OH, YOU REALLY SHOULDN'T HAVE!

THAT'S ALL RIGHT, I'M NOT SHORT OF FISH. LAST SUMMER'S CATCH WAS VERY GOOD... BETTER THAN BUSINESS. THEY'RE MAD ON BOARS IN THIS PLACE.

FISH IS BETTER THAN MEAT. ORTHOPAEDIX WILL MAKE IT COMPULSORY TO EAT FISH ON FRIDAYS.

I LIKE MEAT, MYSELF.

OF COURSE! ORTHOPAEDIX WILL MAKE IT COMPULSORY TO EAT MEAT ON FRIDAYS TOO, AND VICE VERSA.

A GOAT'S MILK, PLEASE!

AND ANOTHER!

POC!

IF HE'S TRYING TO DROWN HIS SORROWS IN GOAT'S MILK, HE MUST HAVE HAD A QUARREL WITH ASTERIX.

A QUARREL WITH ASTERIX...?

23

MY FRIENDS, THESE ARE TROUBLED TIMES!...

WHAT DO WE SEE CONFRONTING US? ON THE ONE HAND, FOREIGNERS TRYING TO TAKE US OVER! ON THE OTHER, A WEAK, APATHETIC CHIEF!

CLUCK?

FRIENDS, I OFFER MYSELF FOR ELECTION! AS YOUR CHIEF, I SHALL BE ENERGETIC!! TOUGH! INFLEXI...

GERIATRIX, LOVEY, COME ON HOME! YOU'LL CATCH YOUR DEATH OF COLD!

!

?

?

THINGS ARE GETTING OUT OF HAND. WHAT NEXT, I WONDER?

AVE!

LISTEN, DO YOU KNOW ANYONE HEREABOUTS WHO USED TO KEEP AN INN AT ARAUSIO?

ORTHOPAEDIX? YES, HE'S LANDLORD OF THE PUB OVER THERE.

THANKS.

25

THE BRACING BREEZE

AVE, ALL!

IT'S THE MAN WHO SOLD ME THE VILLAGE!

'SRIGHT. TREMENSDELIRIUS, AT YOUR SERVICE!

WH... WHAT DO YOU WANT?

A DRINK, FOR A START!

WE ONLY HAVE GOAT'S MILK.

BANG!

AH, SO THAT'S WHY YOU LOOK SO GLUM... BUT I CAN CHANGE ALL THAT.

OH? AND HOW, MAY I ASK?

WELL, I HAVEN'T HAD MUCH LUCK SINCE WE LAST MET... I'VE TRIED ALL SORTS OF JOBS... I EVEN SIGNED ON AS A PIRATE, ONLY UNFORTUNATELY THE PIRATE SHIP GOT SUNK...

NOW I WANT MY VILLAGE BACK. CAESAR GAVE IT TO ME!

BUT YOU SOLD IT TO ME!

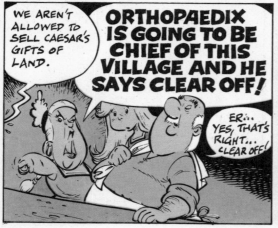

WE AREN'T ALLOWED TO SELL CAESAR'S GIFTS OF LAND.

ORTHOPAEDIX IS GOING TO BE CHIEF OF THIS VILLAGE AND HE SAYS CLEAR OFF!

ER... YES, THAT'S RIGHT... CLEAR OFF!

LOOK HERE, YOU... SEE THIS LITTLE MEMENTO OF MY ARMY SERVICE?

EEEEEK!

26

WHAT RIGHTS DID HE MEAN?

WELL...

OH, IT WAS NOTHING! JUST A COMMON DRUNK. YOU GET THEM IN AN INN NOW AND THEN... THANKS FOR YOUR HELP, ASTERIX.

THE BRACING BREEZE

Z FOR ZAZA... HE MADE A REAL HIT WITH ME!

YOU DON'T THINK THAT LEGIONARY IS GOING TO MAKE TROUBLE, DO YOU? WE OUGHT TO WARN VITALSTATISTIX...

HUH! WHO'S GOING TO LISTEN TO THAT GREAT BLOATED WINESKIN OF A MAN?

YOU'D BETTER GO AND BURY THIS SWORD BEHIND THE HOUSE... WE DON'T WANT ANYONE KNOWING THAT ROMAN WAS HERE. LET'S HOPE ASTERIX KEEPS QUIET.

BUT LATER, AT THE GATES OF THE FORTIFIED ROMAN CAMP OF LAUDANUM...

I'M AN OLD SOLDIER OF THE ROMAN LEGIONS. I'D LIKE TO SEE THE OFFICER COMMANDING THIS GARRISON.

OPTIO!

TREMENSDELIRIUS! WHAT ARE YOU DOING HERE?

CLAUDIUS EGGANLETTUS! YOU DON'T MEAN TO SAY YOU RE-ENLISTED?

THAT'S RIGHT!

I JUST COULDN'T TAKE IT AT NICAEA: PLANTING LETTUCES, WATERING LETTUCES, PICKING LETTUCES... TOO MUCH LIKE WORK. SO I SIGNED ON FOR ANOTHER 20 YEARS AND GOT MY PROMOTION. HOW ABOUT YOU? HOW'S YOUR VILLAGE?

THAT'S THE TROUBLE! I WANT A WORD WITH THE C.O.

FOLLOW ME.

AVE, CENTURION TONSILLITUS! THERE'S AN OLD SOLDIER HERE TO SEE YOU!

SEND HIM IN!

BONG!

IT'S ABOUT THIS GAUL WHO STOLE THE PLOT OF LAND JULIUS CAESAR GAVE ME WHEN I WAS DEMOBBED.

DISGRACEFUL! WE'LL SOON PUT THAT RIGHT! WHEREABOUTS IS YOUR LAND?

NOT FAR OFF... THE FIRST LITTLE VILLAGE YOU COME TO AS YOU GO TOWARDS THE SEA.

WHAT? THE VILLAGE FULL OF MADMEN? CAESAR GAVE YOU THAT VILLAGE FULL OF MADMEN?!

THAT'S RIGHT; I WAS THERE.

WHEN I WANT YOUR OPINION, OPTIO, I'LL ASK FOR IT!

THOSE GAULS ARE TERRIBLE! THEY HAVE DRUIDS WHO GIVE THEM MAGIC POTIONS WHICH MAKE THEM INVINCIBLE!

YOU'D BETTER FORGET THE WHOLE THING... WHY NOT RE-ENLIST LIKE THIS OTHER IDIO... LIKE YOUR FRIEND HERE?

NO! I WANT MY VILLAGE!

CAESAR WOULDN'T LIKE TO THINK OF GAULS GETTING THE BENEFIT OF THE GIFTS HE GIVES HIS OLD SOLDIERS.

THAT'S RIGHT. WHEN I TELL HIM, HE WON'T LIKE IT ONE LITTLE BIT!

OH, ALL RIGHT. WE'LL GET READY... LUCKILY I'VE JUST GOT SOME NEW SECRET WEAPONS IN.

THANKS, O CENTURION!

OH, AND BY THE WAY, OPTIO...

?

YOU'RE NOT AN OPTIO ANY MORE, YOU'RE DEMOTED TO LEGIONARY, SECOND CLASS.

29

33

HELLO, ZAZA.

HELLO, ASTERIX.

WOULD YOU LIKE TO GO INTO THE FOREST AND PICK SOME WILD BOARS?

NO, THANKS.

ASTERIX, I JUST WANTED TO TELL YOU YOU WERE GREAT YESTERDAY! ABSOLUTELY FABULOUS!

OH, ABSOLUTELY FABULOUS, WERE YOU?

I DON'T KNOW ABOUT THAT... WHAT I WANTED TO SAY WAS...

HUH! ABSOLUTELY FABULOUS PEOPLE DON'T HAVE TO EXPLAIN ANYTHING, DO THEY?

EXPLAIN?

YOU LISTEN HERE! WHILE EVERY FOOL IN THE VILLAGE IS TRYING TO GET ELECTED CHIEF, THERE'S SOMETHING REALLY SERIOUS GOING ON! THERE'S THIS ROMAN ABOUT, AND HE'S...

VOTE FOR ME!

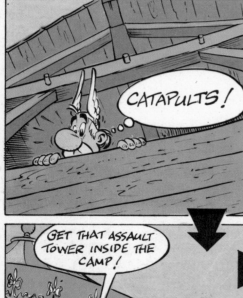

CEN... CEN... CENTURIOOOON!

THERE'S SOMEONE UP ON TOP OF THAT ASSAULT TOWER! IT LOOKS LIKE A GAUL! WE'RE BEING ASSAULTED!

RAISE THE ALARM!

CALM DOWN! WE'VE GOT ENOUGH PROVISIONS TO HOLD OUT FOR A LONG, LONG SIEGE...

COME DOWN FROM THERE, WHOEVER YOU ARE!

IF YOU SAY SO.

I KNOW HIM! HE'S ONE OF THOSE GAULS WHO KEEP KNOCKING BACK THE MAGIC POTION!

HEY, DON'T YOU THINK YOU'RE OVER-REACTING A BIT? THERE'S ONLY ONE OF HIM, AND YOU...

YOU FATHEAD, HE'S FULL OF MAGIC POTION!

I'VE GOT TO GET OUT OF THIS CAMP BEFORE THEY NOTICE ANYTHING FUNNY...

LOOK... LOOK, HE'S RUNNING! AND IF HE'S RUNNING FOR IT, THAT MEANS HE ISN'T FULL OF MAGIC POTION AFTER ALL! CHAAAARGE!

(35)

I'VE GOT TO WARN THEM!

VOTE FOR ME!

WHAT'S UP NOW?

VITALSTATISTIX AND ORTHOPAEDIX HAVE DECIDED TO HAVE A FACE-TO-FACE CONFRONTATION. A PUBLIC DEBATE!

LISTEN, WILL YOU!?

SSH!

SSH!

SSH!

SSH!

SSH!

SSH!

I MUST ASK YOU NOT TO EXCEED YOUR ALLOTTED TIME FOR SPEAKING.

BEFORE WE START, I'D LIKE TO BE SURE THAT OUR UMPIRE IS REALLY IMPARTIAL...

YOUR TIME'S UP!

37

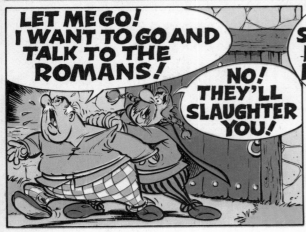

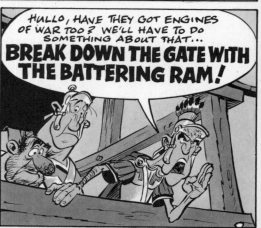

CRAAASH!

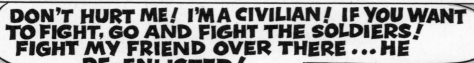

DON'T HURT ME! I'M A CIVILIAN! IF YOU WANT TO FIGHT, GO AND FIGHT THE SOLDIERS! FIGHT MY FRIEND OVER THERE... HE RE-ENLISTED!

I'M NOT GOING TO HURT YOU, FAR FROM IT. I'M GOING TO GIVE YOU BACK YOUR PROPERTY...

Caesar's Gift!

SO NOW ALL YOU'VE GOT TO DO IS DISCUSS THE MATTER WITH CHIEF VITALSTATISTIX AND HIS MEN!

PAF!

HEY, WAIT A MINUTE! YOU WOULDN'T DO A THING LIKE THAT TO AN OLD FRIEND, WOULD YOU?

COME ON, LET'S GO HOME!

SOON AFTERWARDS...

RIGHT, LEGIONARY EGGANLETTUS, JUST SWEEP THIS LOT UP, AND WE WILL NOT REFER TO IT AGAIN!

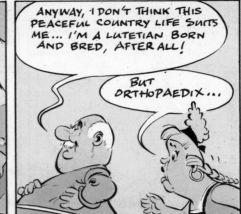

OBELIX IS FRIENDS WITH ME AGAIN!

IN FACT, EVERYONE IS FRIENDS AGAIN. UNDER THE STARRY SKY, ALL PARTIES ARE RE-UNITED AROUND THE TABLE. ALL PARTIES... FOR WE MUST NOT FORGET THAT THIS HAPPENED VERY LONG AGO, ABOUT 50 BC, AND IN THOSE DAYS SUCH MATTERS WERE NOT SO VERY IMPORTANT...

VOTE FOR ME!

THE END
6-74